A Cuddle
for Claude

Text and illustrations copyright © 2000 by David Wojtowycz

All rights reserved.

CIP Data is available.

Published in the United States 2001 by Dutton Children's Books,

a division of Penguin Putnam Books for Young Readers

345 Hudson Street, New York, New York 10014

www.penguinputnam.com

Originally published in Great Britain 2000

by David & Charles Children's Books, London

Typography by Carolyn T. Fucile

Printed in Belgium

First American Edition

ISBN 0-525-46691-6

2 4 6 8 10 9 7 5 3

A Cuddle for Claude

DAVID WOJTOWYCZ

DUTTON CHILDREN'S BOOKS · NEW YORK

Claude woke up from his afternoon nap.
In his sleep he had been hugging his blanket.
Now he wanted a real cuddle from his mom.

So he went to find her.

Mom had her arms full of groceries.
"Hello, dear," she said. "Are you up already?"
When he asked for a hug, she kissed him
on the forehead.
"I'll give you a great big cuddle, Claude.
I just have a few things to finish first.
Why don't you look at a book,
and I'll come as soon as I can."

Claude went to the bookshelf and took out his favorite book. He read and read—at least *four* pages.

GOLDILOCKS

BEDTIME BOOK FOR BEARS

GRIZZLY ADAMS

POLAR BEAR handbook

Then he went to find Mom.
She was mixing some sticky stuff
in a bowl.
"Have you finished reading already?"
she said, glancing at the clock.
"I'd give you a cuddle, Claude,
but my hands are all covered with dough.
Why don't you draw a picture,
and I'll come and cuddle you
just as soon as 1 can."

Claude sat at his desk.
He drew and drew
until there was no paper left.

Then he went to find Mom.
"Have you finished your picture already?"
she asked as she took her baking out
of the oven. "I'd give you a cuddle, Claude,
but this tray is very hot.
Why don't you do your puzzle,
and I'll come and cuddle you
just as soon as I can."

Claude pulled out his best jigsaw puzzle.
He put all the pieces together.
They didn't look quite right,
but he was sure Mom *must*
be ready by now.

But she wasn't.
"Have you finished your puzzle already?"

"I just have to finish this, Claude, then I *promise* I'll come and cuddle you."

Claude was fed up. He'd read *four* pages
of his book, drawn loads of pictures,
and done his most difficult jigsaw puzzle—well, almost.
But Mom still hadn't given him his cuddle.

There could be
only one explanation—
she didn't love him anymore!
He packed his toys into his blanket.

Mom finished at last and called to Claude,
but he was nowhere to be seen.

Then she spotted a trail of toys leading into the garden.

Claude was sitting on his blanket
under the big tree.
"What are you doing out here?"
asked Mom.
Claude looked very sad.
"Oh, Claude," said Mom,
and she took him by the hand.

"I'm sorry I was too busy to cuddle you,"
Mom said. "I just wanted everything
to be ready for your surprise."
Mom showed Claude the table.
It was laid out with a fancy afternoon snack,
including Claude's favorite freshly
baked cookies. Just then the doorbell rang.

"Surprise!" someone cried
as she popped her head around the door.
It was Grandma!

"Now can *I* have a cuddle?" asked Mom.
"Me too!" laughed Grandma.
And they all gave each other the biggest

cuddle

they could!

FOR MY MUM XXX